There are many versions of this classic tale. In the tradition of the storyteller, each one is uniquely different.

— *Jane Belk Moncure*

© 1988 Parramón Ediciones, S. A.
Printed in Spain by Sirven Gràfic, S. A.
© Alexander Publishers' Marketing
and The Child's World, Inc.: English
edition, 1988.
ISBN 0-89565-458-X
L.D.: B-37.953-88

COLLODI
Pinocchio

Illustration: Agustí Asensio
Adaptation: Eduard José

Retold by Jane Belk Moncure

 The Child's World, Inc.

Long ago, in a village far away, there lived a kind old puppet maker named Gepetto. The old man lived all alone except for a cat and a goldfish.

"I am so lonely," said Gepetto one rainy day. "I need someone to talk to."

Then it was that Gepetto had an idea. "I will make a puppet just for me," he said. "A puppet to keep me company!" Gepetto went right to work. When he finished, he was so happy with the puppet that he wanted to give it a name.

"I will call you Pinocchio," he said. "My, you look like a real little boy. How I wish you were. You could be my son!"

Now the Good Blue Fairy heard Gepetto's wish, and she felt sorry for him. So, that night, she touched Pinocchio with her magic wand.

"Wake up," she said, and Pinocchio blinked his eyes.

"You are to be Gepetto's son." said the fairy.
"Be very good to him and do as he says, for no
one will love you as much as he."

Then the fairy saw a little cricket hiding in a
box.

"And you, Cricket, help Pinocchio as best you
can. Stay with him always and keep him out of
trouble."

Then, in a twinkle, the Blue Fairy was gone.

When the old puppet maker awoke, he couldn't believe his eyes.

"A little boy! A real little son! Oh! I am the happiest puppet maker in all the world!" he cried.

Gepetto bought Pinocchio warm winter clothes and new books for school. In fact, he spent all of his money on his little wooden son.

Now, Pinocchio did not much like school. He thought it was silly. But Cricket told him, "If you do not go to school, you will be the silliest boy of all!"

"You're right," said Pinocchio. "I will learn very quickly. Then I will go to work and earn money for Gepetto."

And off he went to school.

Pinocchio had not gone far when he heard music. He followed the sound and found a crowd of people outside an old theater. A sign said, "Puppet Show! Come One, Come All!"

"Puppets!" thought Pinocchio. "I can't miss this!" So, forgetting all about school, Pinocchio sold his books to buy a ticket for the puppet show.

When the puppeteer saw Pinocchio, he had a nasty idea.

"Well, well," he thought, "a puppet who moves without strings! If I had him in my show, I could get rich!"

The puppeteer grabbed Pinocchio and threw him into his puppet box. Poor Pinocchio began to cry.

"Now I will never see my father again," Pinocchio cried. "And he has no money and is all alone. He needs me."

When the puppeteer heard Pinocchio crying, he thought of his own father. He felt so sorry for Pinocchio, he let him go free. He even gave Pinocchio five coins to take home to Gepetto.

"Hurry home," said the puppeteer. "And from now on, be careful!"

"I will," said Pinocchio. And away he went.

But as he walked home, Pinocchio played with his five gold coins and began to think.

"Five gold coins are not many coins. If I could turn these five coins into fifty, then I'd be rich! Gepetto would be so proud of me!"

From behind the fence, a sneaky fox and a wicked cat were watching Pinocchio. They looked at the gold coins with greedy eyes.

"We will trick that silly wooden boy," said Fox.

"Those five gold coins will soon be ours," said Cat.

Then, jumping out from behind the fence, Fox spoke. "Dear boy," he said, "we know how you can make your five gold coins into fifty. Just bury them in this magic snow. Then when you come back, you will find a big tree full of gold coins."

"Yes," said Cat. "Gold coins."

Pinocchio did just as he was told. You can
imagine what happened. When he came back,
looking for the money tree, it was not there.
In fact, all his money was gone! The fox and
cat had stolen his treasure. Poor Pinocchio was
angry and cold.

"You must be careful who you trust," said
Cricket.

"Go away, silly cricket!" yelled Pinocchio.
And he ran straight home, crying all the way.

Later that night, the Blue Fairy came for a visit.

"You have made me sad," said the fairy. "Cricket tells me you have been a bad boy."

"That's not true!" yelled Pinocchio. "I'm the best puppet ever!"

Then a strange thing happened. Pinocchio felt his nose growing.

"Pinocchio," said the fairy, "where did you go today?"

"I went to school," said Pinocchio. Oops! Pinocchio felt his nose growing longer still.

"Where are your books?" asked the fairy.

"I . . . I . . . lost them at school," he answered. Oops! Again Pinocchio felt his nose grow longer.

"What is happening?" asked Pinocchio. "Why is my nose growing?" He was very scared.

"You are telling lies," said the Blue Fairy. "Each time you tell a lie, your nose grows."

"Please make my nose short again," said Pinocchio. "I will tell the truth from now on."

"First you must find your dear father," said the fairy. "He went looking for you and now is lost at sea."

"Oh no!" said Pinocchio. "My father is lost at sea, all because of me! I must go and find him at once!"

Pinocchio and Cricket started on the journey but couldn't go very far. A big storm arose and great waves crashed on the shore.

"We will have to wait until this storm has passed," said Pinocchio. "Then we will find a boat and look for my father."

While they were waiting, a peddler came by. He was carrying a wagon load of boys and girls. They were all laughing and singing.

"Come along with us," they called. "We are going to Toyland where everyone plays all day and all night."

"Don't go," warned Cricket. "It may be a trick."

"Don't be silly," said Pinocchio. "I will only go for a short time. I will come back when the storm is over to look for Gepetto."

Pinocchio jumped on the wagon, and away he went.

Toyland was a great place, full of music, games, and candy. Pinocchio was having a wonderful time, playing and eating. But suddenly, he felt strange. When he looked into a mirror, he saw that his ears had grown long like a donkey's ears!

"What is happening?" he cried, for he was very scared.

"Ha, ha!" said the peddler. "I have fed you magic food to turn you into a donkey. Now you will pull my wagon for the rest of your life!"

"No! No!" cried Pinocchio, and he ran as fast as his legs could take him. But as he ran, he felt a long tail growing. "No! No! I don't want to be a donkey!" Pinocchio cried.

The peddler chased Pinocchio all the way back to the sea.

"Jump!" cried Cricket. And Pinocchio jumped right into the waves. As soon as he hit the cold water, he became himself again. But his troubles were far from over because right in front of him was a giant whale.

"Watch out!" cried Cricket.

It was too late. The whale opened his jaws wide and swallowed the little wooden puppet.

But when Pinocchio tumbled down into the belly of the giant whale, who should he find but his very own father, Gepetto.

"Father!" he cried. "I have found you at last."

"And I have found you, my son," said Gepetto. "I have been looking for you for a very long time!"

"Now we must get out of here," said Pinocchio. "I have an idea!"

He tickled the whale, and the whale sneezed— such a sneeze that it blew Pinocchio, his father, and Cricket right up onto the beach!

Soon they were safe at home.

"What has happened to your nose?" asked Gepetto.

Pinocchio told his father the truth about what a bad son he had been. As soon as he had told Gepetto everything, his nose grew short again.

"I want to be a good son to you from now on," said Pinocchio.

Just then, POOF! The Blue Fairy appeared.

"You have learned your lesson at last," she said. "For that, I will give you a gift." And she touched Pinocchio with her magic wand. Pinocchio's body became soft, and he felt his skin.

"I'm a boy!" he cried. "A real live boy!"

And from that day on, Pinocchio and Gepetto lived happily together, and the old puppet maker was lonely no more.